This book belongs to:

_____

Lily SAYS NO!

Written by Kelly Eastmond-Jeffrey

Illustrated by Princess of the Most High S.B.S

Lily Says No!

First Printed in the United Kingdom 2020

Published by Conscious Dreams Publishing
www.consciousdreamspublishing.com

Illustrated by Princess of the Most High S.B.S

Edited by Daniella Blechner

Typeset by Oksana Kosovan

ISBN: 978-1-913674-18-2

DEDICATION

Dedicated to Jessica Paige Sandford and
Jeanette Lesley Baxter (nee)

"Always in my heart".

I live in a BIG house with my mum and my step dad. I have a big brother called Tom. My mum has a baby in her tummy.

I am seven years old and I am in Year 3 at Longville Primary School. Sometimes, after school, Mum takes me and Tom to the park and we all have lots of fun together.

My step-dad's name is Mark. He works in a sweetie factory and gives me lots of yummy sweets all the time, sometimes I eat so many, my tummy hurts!

At bedtime, Mum usually reads me a story before tucking me in for the night, but lately she has been so tired, so now Mark does it instead.

I wish my mum would tuck me in again. Mark keeps telling me to keep secrets. He said Mum would get upset with me if I tell her... I don't like Mark anymore.

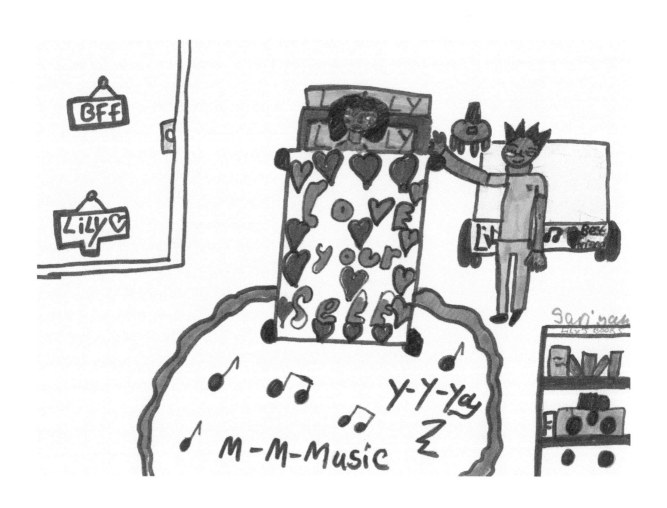

Mark doesn't read bedtime stories to me anymore. He just always wants to play his special tickle game where he touches me somewhere and I have to tell him what it is. Every time I get it right, I get a kiss and cuddle. Mum said I am being a good girl when I am nice to Mark, but I really don't like it.

Sariyah

I don't want Mark to come into my room anymore! I don't like him. He hurts me. I don't want to play his special games and I don't want his kisses and cuddles. I just want my mum back.

Mum asked me how I was getting along with Mark today. I told her what had been happening in my bedroom with Mark. I told her about all the secret games I had to do with him. Mum asked me what games we were playing that made me feel uncomfortable. I told her about the tickle game. I told her how, at first, it was okay because it was funny, but then.. Mark tickled up my legs. Mum looked sad. She told me she had no idea and that she would sort it out. She gave me a cuddle and a kiss - It felt nice, I felt safe with my mum.

At bedtime, Mum came into my room tucked me into bed and read me a story, just like she used to. She kissed me on my forehead and told me to go to sleep, and then as if by magic, I did just that! I woke up suddenly in the night. There was shouting. I was scared, so I got out of bed to see what was going on. As I walked towards my bedroom door, I heard Mum screaming at Mark to get out. A door slammed and I heard Mum crying. I went to see my mum and sat beside her on the bed. I told my mum I was sorry. She told me I had nothing to be sorry about and that what Mark did to me was wrong.

The next day, when I woke up, Mum helped me get ready for school. I had coco pops for breakfast and then Mum took me to school in her new car.

Sariyah

We got to school a bit early. Tom saw his friends so asked if he could go to them. Mum said yes but told me to wait a minute as she wanted to talk to me about something. She said that what Mark had been doing to me was wrong. People who hurt children by touching their private parts are bad and they should be in prison. Mark did something bad and Mum was going to make sure that he goes to prison too so that he can't hurt any other children. She told me I was a very brave and strong little girl and that she was sorry that she did not notice what was going on to stop it earlier. She told me it wasn't my fault as I am a child. She said he was wrong because he knew it is wrong and he still did it. She promised that she would make sure he never hurts me again.

MESSAGE FROM THE AUTHOR

If someone you know is hurting you or doing something you don't feel comfortable with, do something. Speak up and say NO!

Talk to an adult you know you can trust or phone Childline on 0800 11 11.

If you tell a teacher in school, they have to protect you by law. They will act on your behalf to make sure you are kept safe and the person that is hurting you will be in trouble with the police to make sure they cannot hurt you or other little girls or boys ever again.

THANK YOUS

I would like to say a huge thank you to all my family and close friends,
who over the years have encouraged and supported me
in following my dream to publish my work.

I would also like to Thank my illustrator:
Princess Of The Most High S.B.S for all her hard work and Queen SF
for allowing me to work with her – You have prompted and encouraged
your daughter to do her best and stay focused.
I am greatly appreciative.

And last but most definitely not least –
I would like to say a Huge thank you to: Karen Eastmond
and Sharon Fevrier as well as Daniella Blechner and Oksana Kosovan
from Conscious Dreams Publishing.

ABOUT THE AUTHOR

Kelly has always worked with people of all ages, she is a qualified and experienced care assistant and play worker who loves books. She loved books as a child and always wanted to be an author one day.

Kelly worked with other residents to create a local community charity. They had family day trips, events and projects and even looked after senior citizens with carol singing at Christmas, tea dances and day trips. Kelly still volunteers in East London to give children and families with little money a happier life

She is the 2nd youngest of eight siblings; has two children; four nephews; eight nieces; two great-nieces; three great-nephews and five God-daughters. Kelly loves having a big family and loves to socialise. She also has a great passion for music, nature, art, cooking and travelling.

ABOUT THE ILLUSTRATOR

Princess of the Most High S.BS aka, Sariyah, is ten years old. Her hobbies include vlogging, cooking and entertaining. She loves gymnastics, ballet and tap dancing. Sariyah found it easier to understand this story when she asked questions.

She thinks it is important to have stories like these that encourage conversations, awareness and help protect children. Sariyah says, "It is important that these messages are delivered to children, so that no more children are harmed".

Sariyah is inspired by her parents and Kelly for giving her this opportunity and she intends to continue reading, writing and Illustrating.

Conscious Dreams
PUBLISHING

Be the author of your own destiny

Find out about our authors, events, services
and how you too can get your book journey started.

 Conscious Dreams Publishing

 @DreamsConscious

 @consciousdreamspublishing

 Daniella Blechner

 www.consciousdreamspublishing.com

 info@consciousdreamspublishing.com

Let's connect